HANS CHRISTIAN ANDERSEN

THE
LITTLE MATCH GIRL

Adapted and illustrated by
JERRY PINKNEY

PUFFIN BOOKS

PUFFIN BOOKS
Published by the Penguin Group
Penguin Putnam Books for Young Readers,
345 Hudson Street, New York, New York 10014, U.S.A.
Penguin Books Ltd, 80 Strand, London WC2R ORL, England
Penguin Books Australia Ltd, Ringwood, Victoria, Australia
Penguin Books Canada Ltd, 10 Alcorn Avenue, Toronto, Ontario, Canada M4V 3B2
Penguin Books (N.Z.) Ltd, 182-190 Wairau Road, Auckland 10, New Zealand

Penguin Books Ltd, Registered Offices: Harmondsworth, Middlesex, England

First published in the United States of America by Phyllis Fogelman Books, an imprint of Penguin
Putnam Books for Young Readers, 1999
Published by Puffin Books, a division of Penguin Putnam Books for Young Readers, 2002

1 3 5 7 9 10 8 6 4 2

THE LIBRARY OF CONGRESS HAS CATALOGED THE PHYLLIS FOGELMAN BOOKS EDITION AS FOLLOWS:
Pinkney, Jerry.
The little match girl / by Hans Christian Andersen; adapted and illustrated by Jerry Pinkney.—1st ed.
p. cm.
Summary: An American child of the early 1920s who sells matches is visited by visions that bring
some beauty to her brief, tragic life.
ISBN: 0-8037-2314-8 (hc)
[1. Fairy tales.] I. Andersen, H. C. (Hans Christian), 1805-1875. Adaptation/translation of Lille pige
med svovlstikkerne. English. II. Title.
PZ8.P575Li 1999 [E]—dc21 99-13814 CIP
The full-color artwork has been prepared using pencil, gouache, and watercolor on paper.

Puffin Books ISBN 0-14-230188-4

Printed in the United States of America

To Gloria Jean
for her vision and help in revisiting this time-honored classic

Photographs from the early 20th century show children in some of our
most affluent cities on the streets peddling vegetables, flowers, gum,
and matches. Their faces have stayed with me and haunt
my visual memory.

J.P.

It was cold in the small, cramped attic of the tenement where a family of five children was at work making artificial flowers. The wind whistled through the room, try as they might to stuff the biggest cracks with rags and straw. One of the children, who had an especially graceful way about her, was sent out to sell flowers and matches in the city. It was late in the wintry afternoon of New Year's Eve as the poor little girl walked along the icy streets.

She had had slippers on when she left home, but they were not much good, for they were so huge. They had last been worn by her mother, and they fell off the girl's feet when she was running across the avenue to avoid an automobile and a carriage that had nearly collided.

So the poor little girl went on with nothing but torn stockings on her numb feet. She carried a quantity of matches in a tray and the flowers in a basket. As she trudged along, she marveled at the many wonderful things for sale, things that the little girl could never have imagined. And there was a most delicious odor of roast goose in the streets, for it was New Year's Eve. She could not forget that.

Nobody had bought anything from her as the afternoon turned into evening; nobody had even given her a coin. The child was hungry and trembling from the bitter cold, and she looked the picture of misery.

The little girl longed to go home, but she could not, as she had not sold any of her matches or flowers.

Her father would beat her; besides, it was almost as cold at home as it was here. She walked on until she found a corner that seemed to offer protection from the wind, but she was colder than ever.

Her little hands and feet were almost stiff with cold. She thought
perhaps a match would do some good. But did she dare take one from
the tray and strike it on the wall to warm her fingers? She pulled one
out, and with a *rrsschh,* it blazed into life. It burned with a bright,
clear flame, just like a little candle when she held her hand around it.
It gave off a very strange light too.

It seemed to the little girl that she was sitting in front of a big stove with polished brass feet and handles. There was a splendid fire blazing in it and warming her so beautifully; but just as she was stretching her feet to warm them . . .

the blaze went out, the stove vanished, and she was left sitting with the end of the burned-out match in her hand.

She struck a new one. It burned, it blazed up, and where the light fell, the wall became transparent, and she saw a marvelous feast spread out before her. The table was spread with a white cloth and pretty china; a roast goose stuffed with apples and chestnuts was steaming on it. There was another table filled with cookies and desserts of all kinds. The little girl's mouth watered as she gazed at these delicacies. The match went out, and there was nothing to be seen but the bare brick wall.

Again, she lit another. This time she was sitting next to a lovely
Christmas tree, surrounded by beautiful clothes and toys—all the
things she had seen only in shop windows. Thousands of lighted
candles gleamed upon the tree's branches. The little girl stretched
out both her hands toward them—then out went the match. The
Christmas candles rose higher and higher, till she saw that they were
only the twinkling stars.

One of them fell and made a bright streak of light across the sky.
Someone is dying, thought the little girl; for her old grandmother,
the only person who had ever been kind to her, used to say, "When a
star falls, a soul is going up to God."

Now she struck another match against the wall, and this time it was her grandmother who appeared in the circle of flame. She saw her quite clearly and distinctly, looking so gentle and loving.

She lit still another, and this time she was with her grandmother,
just as they had been so many times before. How real it all seemed to be.

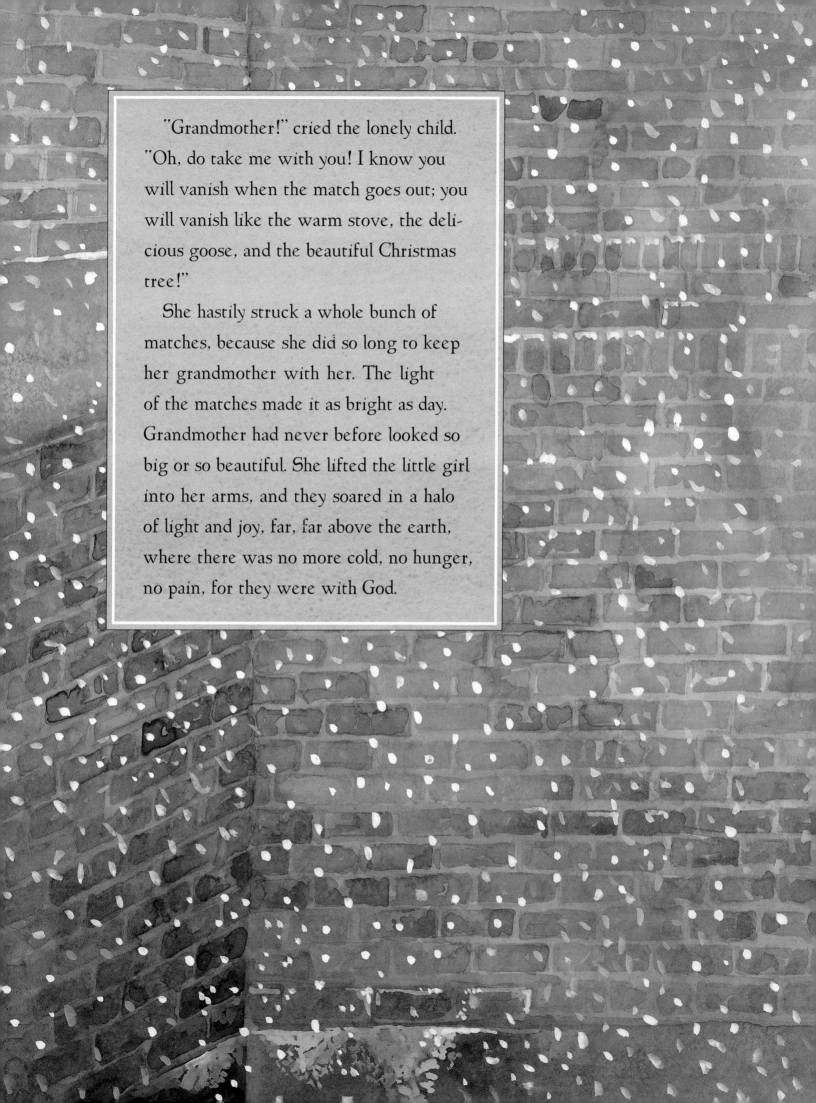

"Grandmother!" cried the lonely child.
"Oh, do take me with you! I know you
will vanish when the match goes out; you
will vanish like the warm stove, the delicious goose, and the beautiful Christmas
tree!"

She hastily struck a whole bunch of
matches, because she did so long to keep
her grandmother with her. The light
of the matches made it as bright as day.
Grandmother had never before looked so
big or so beautiful. She lifted the little girl
into her arms, and they soared in a halo
of light and joy, far, far above the earth,
where there was no more cold, no hunger,
no pain, for they were with God.

In the cold morning light the poor little girl sat there in the corner with a smile on her face—dead. Frozen to death on the last night of the old year. When the people of the city finally arose on New Year's Day, they discovered the little body still sitting with the ends of the burned-out matches in her hand. The flowers had been scattered by the frigid night wind across the sidewalk and into the street.

She must have tried to warm herself, some said.

But no one imagined what beautiful visions she had seen,
nor into what glory she had entered with her grandmother
in the New Year.